CARTER HIGH
M Y S T E R I E S

THE
MISSING TEST
Mystery

By Eleanor Robins

SADDLEBACK
EDUCATIONAL PUBLISHING

CARTER HIGH
MYSTERIES

SADDLEBACK
EDUCATIONAL PUBLISHING
www.sdlback.com

ISBN-13: 978-1-61651-566-9
ISBN-10: 1-61651-566-X
eBook: 978-1-61247-134-1

Printed in Guangzhou, China
NOR/0813/CA21301539

17 16 15 14 13   3 4 5 6 7

Chapter 1

It was Monday. Drake was at football practice. Drake was the starting quarterback. The big game was on Friday night. Drake could hardly wait.

Coach Grant called to Drake. He said, "Come over here, Drake. I need to talk to you now."

Drake hurried over to the coach.

The coach asked, "How are you doing, Drake?"

"Fine," Drake said. But why did the coach ask him that?

"No problems here at school?" Coach Grant asked.

"No. No problems, Coach," Drake said.

But that wasn't true. He did have one problem.

Coach Grant said, "I talked to Mrs. Wray today."

The coach didn't sound pleased.

Drake knew he was in trouble. Mrs. Wray was his history teacher.

Drake asked, "What did Mrs. Wray say to you?"

But Drake was sure he knew what Mrs. Wray said.

The coach said, "Mrs. Wray said you are failing history. Why didn't you tell me about it?"

Drake didn't want Coach Grant to know. But Drake knew he couldn't tell Coach Grant that.

So Drake said, "It isn't a big deal. I can improve my grade before the end of the semester."

"It's a big deal to me, Drake. And it should be to you, too. I want you to improve your grade now, not later. Mrs. Wray said you have a test on Friday morning. Pass that test if you want to play on Friday night," Coach Grant said.

"I have to play on Friday night. That's our big game," Drake said.

"You don't have to play on Friday night, Drake. I can start Caleb," Coach Grant said.

Caleb was the back-up quarterback.

"But Caleb doesn't play as well as I do," Drake said.

"Caleb is passing all of his classes. You aren't passing all of your classes. Get back to practice," Coach Grant said.

Drake jogged back over to the other players. Caleb ran over to him.

Caleb asked, "What did Coach Grant say to you?"

Drake told Caleb what happened.

Caleb said, "Then you'd better study for that test and pass. Or Coach Grant won't let you play on Friday night. You need to play. I want to win. And we might not win if I have to start."

Drake thought they might not win, too. Caleb wasn't a good quarterback.

"Don't worry. I'll study. And I'll pass the test," Drake said.

Drake knew he would study. And he thought he would pass if he studied a lot. He just didn't like to study history.

Drake threw some passes to two players. Caleb threw some passes.

Drake worked hard for the rest of the practice. But he was thinking about what Coach Grant said about his test.

Coach Grant blew his whistle. All of the boys stopped what they were doing. They ran over to Coach Grant.

Coach Grant said, "Time is up for today. All of you worked hard today. Study tonight. Get a lot of sleep. And be ready to work hard tomorrow."

Some of the players ran to the gym.

Coach Grant said, "Wait a minute, Drake."

Drake waited to see what the coach wanted to say.

Coach Grant said, "One more thing, Drake. I want to see your test before the game starts. Bring it to me so I'll know you passed."

"Mrs. Wray might not grade my test before the game. So I might not be able to bring it to you. Will you still let me play?" Drake asked.

"Mrs. Wray said she'll grade your test on Friday. Don't forget to bring your test to me, Drake. And don't lose it. I must see your test. And the test must have a passing grade, or you don't play," Coach Grant said.

"I'll be sure to bring it. And I'll have a passing grade," Drake said.

"Good, Drake. See you tomorrow," Coach Grant said.

Coach Grant didn't trust Drake to tell the truth about his grade. And that upset Drake. But he knew why the coach didn't trust him. And it was his fault. He was failing history. And he should have told the coach that.

Drake turned around to run to the gym. Caleb was right behind him. And Drake almost bumped into Caleb.

Chapter 2

It was Friday morning. Drake was at the bus stop. He read his history notes.

His friend, Logan, walked up to the bus stop.

They both lived at Grayson Apartments. And they rode the same bus to school.

Logan asked, "What are you doing now, Drake?"

"I'm studying for my history test," Drake said.

"Why are you doing it now? You should have studied last night."

"I did. I studied a lot. But I want to study some more. I have to pass the test," Drake said.

"You'd better pass it. We need to win that game tonight. And you have to play," Logan said.

The bus came. The two boys got on the bus.

Drake sat with Logan. Drake wanted to study some more. So they didn't talk. Drake studied all the way to school.

The bus arrived at school. Logan said, "See you later, Drake. Good luck on the test." The boys got off the bus.

Logan hurried off. And Drake knew why he did.

Logan had seen a girl he was trying to date. And he wanted to talk to her before school started.

Caleb ran up to Drake.

Caleb said, "This is a big game tonight.

I hope you studied for the test. Did you?"

"Yeah. A lot more than I wanted to study," Drake said.

"Do you think you'll pass the test?" Caleb asked.

Drake said, "Yeah. I should pass. But I won't know for sure until I see the test."

"Glad you studied," Caleb said. Then Caleb walked off.

The bell rang. Drake put away his notes. And he hurried into the school.

Drake was glad when his first two classes were over. Now it was time for his history class.

Drake hurried into the classroom. He went to his desk and sat down.

The bell rang to start class.

Mrs. Wray called the roll.

Then Mrs. Wray said, "Time to start the test. Put your books and notes away. And have your pens ready."

Mrs. Wray started to pass out the tests. Drake could hardly wait to get his test. He started it as soon as he got it.

He worked very hard on it all period. He finished just as the bell rang.

Mrs. Wray said, "Give me your tests as you go out the door. I hope all of you did well."

Drake was sure he did well. He thought the test was easy. But maybe that was because he'd studied a long time for it.

Drake hurried over to Mrs. Wray. He gave his test to her. Then he asked, "When are you going to grade my test? I have to show Coach Grant my grade. Then he'll let me play tonight."

Mrs. Wray said, "Coach Grant told me about that. I'm going to lunch now. But I'll grade your test as soon as I get back. Come by after school. I'll give your test to you. Then you can take it to Coach Grant."

"Thanks," Drake said.

Drake went out into the hall.

Logan hurried out of Mr. Zane's room. Mr. Zane's room was next door to Mrs. Wray's room.

Both boys had Mr. Zane for science. But not at the same time.

Logan asked, "How did you do on the test? Do you think you passed it?"

"Yeah," Drake said.

"Great. Then you can play tonight. See you later," Logan said. Then Logan hurried down the hall.

Drake walked to his math class. Miss Ortiz was his math teacher.

Miss Ortiz had asked Drake to get a book from Mr. Zane. And she'd asked Drake to bring the book to her. But Drake was thinking about his test. So he forgot to get the book.

Caleb called to him. Caleb said, "Wait, Drake."

Drake stopped. He waited for Caleb. Caleb hurried up to him.

Caleb asked, "How do you think you did on your test?"

"I think I got a high C. Or maybe a B," Drake said.

Caleb said, "Great. Now you can play tonight. And I won't have to start. And I'm sure we'll win if you play."

Drake was sure they would win, too. Or at least they had a good chance. As long as he was playing and not Caleb.

Caleb said, "Oh, no. I just thought of something."

"What?" Drake asked.

"Mrs. Wray might not grade your test before the game. And Coach Grant won't let you play," Caleb said.

"Mrs. Wray knows I need my test back

before the game. She's going to lunch now. But she'll grade it as soon as she gets back from lunch. And I can get my test after school," Drake said.

Caleb said, "Great. I need to go now. I don't want to be late for lunch. See you later."

Caleb seemed to be in a hurry. So why did he take time to ask Drake about the test?

Chapter 3

Drake hurried into his math class. He was almost late. He sat down next to his friend, Jack. Jack lived at Grayson Apartments, too.

"How do you think you did on your test?" Jack asked.

"I'm sure I passed," Drake said.

"Way to go," Jack said.

The bell rang. So Miss Ortiz started the class.

The students worked for about 20 minutes.

Then Miss Ortiz asked, "Drake, did you get the book from Mr. Zane? I need it now."

That was the first time Drake had thought about the book all morning.

"No, Miss Ortiz. I forgot to get the book. Do you want me to go and get it now?" Drake asked.

"Yes, Drake. And hurry."

Drake quickly got up. He went out into the hall. Then he hurried to Mr. Zane's room.

Mr. Zane was teaching his class. His door was open. But Drake still knocked on the door.

Mr. Zane looked over at Drake. He said, "Come in, Drake."

Drake walked into the room. He said, "I'm sorry to bother you, Mr. Zane. But I need that book for Miss Ortiz."

"I have a class to teach, Drake. You should have gotten the book before my class started," Mr. Zane said.

"I know, Mr. Zane. But I forgot to get it then," Drake said.

Mr. Zane gave the book to Drake. And Drake went back out into the hall.

Drake knew he should hurry back to class. But Mrs. Wray's classroom was next door. Maybe she was back from lunch. And maybe she had graded his test. He could hardly wait to find out what grade he got.

He could quickly go into Mrs. Wray's room and find out. It wouldn't take him long to do that. He could be gone from his math class for a few more minutes. That would be okay.

Drake quickly went to Mrs. Wray's door. He looked into the room. But he didn't see Mrs. Wray.

Drake stood there for a minute. He wanted to look on Mrs. Wray's desk. But he knew he shouldn't do that.

He turned around to go back to Miss Ortiz's class.

Drake saw Mr. Zane. Mr. Zane was standing in the doorway of his classroom. Mr. Zane was looking right at Drake.

Mr. Zane said, "I thought you'd gone back to your class. You shouldn't be here. You should be in your class."

"I'm on my way now," Drake said.

Drake hurried back to his math class. He gave the book to Miss Ortiz.

Miss Ortiz said, "I didn't think you would be gone that long, Drake."

"Sorry. I tried to hurry," Drake said.

Miss Ortiz opened the book. She showed the class pictures of some buildings. And she told the students how math had helped build the buildings.

There was a knock at the door. Mrs. Wray came in. She seemed upset. She said, "I'm sorry to bother your class, Miss Ortiz.

But I need to speak with Drake now."

All of the students looked at Drake.

Did Mrs. Wray come to tell Drake his grade? Drake didn't think she did. She seemed upset. And he didn't think his grade would upset her. Even if he got a bad grade. But he was still sure he got a good grade.

So why did Mrs. Wray need to see him now? Drake wasn't sure he wanted to know.

Chapter 4

Drake went to Mrs. Wray's room.

When they got there, Mrs. Wray quickly closed the door. Then she looked at Drake.

She said, "I need your test, Drake."

That surprised Drake very much. How could Mrs. Wray forget he gave the test to her?

Drake said, "But I gave my test to you. And we talked about when you would grade it."

"But your test is gone, Drake," Mrs. Wray said.

"Gone? What do you mean it's gone?" Drake asked.

How could his test be gone? It couldn't just walk off.

Mrs. Wray sat down at her desk. Then she said, "Someone took the test. It was on my desk when I went to lunch. But it wasn't there when I came back. And I could see someone had moved the tests."

"But it wasn't me. Why would I take my test?" Drake asked.

"Because you knew you didn't do well on it. And you didn't want me to grade it," Mrs. Wray said.

Drake said, "But I did do well. I told you I knew I did. So why would I take my test?"

"But who else would want to take it?" Mrs. Wray asked.

"I don't know. But I didn't take it," Drake said.

"I know you went into my room while I was at lunch. Mr. Zane told me you did. You knew I wouldn't be there. So why did you go into my room?" Mrs. Wray asked.

"I thought maybe you were back. And that you had graded my test. But I didn't go into your room. I only went to the door," Drake said.

"You're the only one who was seen at my door, Drake. And you're the only one who might want to take the test. I'll have to tell Coach Grant about this. And I'll have to tell Mr. Glenn," Mrs. Wray said.

Mr. Glenn was the principal.

"So give me the test now, Drake. It will be better for you if you do," Mrs. Wray said.

"But I didn't take it," Drake said.

Mrs. Wray said, "I hope you didn't, Drake. But I can think of no one else who would want the test."

And Drake could think of no one else who would want to take it either.

But Drake didn't take the test. And Mrs. Wray didn't believe him.

What was he going to do?

Mrs. Wray said, "Now you need to get back to class, Drake. But I'm sure Coach Grant will want to talk to you later. And Mr. Glenn will want to talk to you, too."

Mrs. Wray really thought Drake was lying to her.

Would Coach Grant and Mr. Glenn think he was lying, too?

Chapter 5

Drake opened the classroom door. And he went back into Miss Ortiz's room. He was upset.

All of the students were looking at him. Drake knew they wondered why Mrs. Wray wanted to see him. And he knew they were sure he'd done something wrong.

Drake tried to do his work. But he couldn't keep his mind on it. He was glad it was almost time for his class to be over.

The bell rang.

Drake quickly got up. And he walked to the door. Jack walked with him. Jack looked at Drake.

Jack asked, "What did Mrs. Wray want? Did you fail your test?"

"No. It's a lot worse than that. My test is missing," Drake said.

Jack asked, "Missing? How could your test be missing? It couldn't just walk off. What did you do with it? Didn't you give it to Mrs. Wray?"

"Yeah," Drake said.

"Then Mrs. Wray just forgot where she put it," Jack said.

"Mrs. Wray left it on her desk. And then she went to lunch. My test wasn't there when she came back from lunch. She thinks I took it. She thinks I was sure I got a bad grade. And that's why she thinks I took it," Drake said.

"But you didn't take your test. You wouldn't do that. Mrs. Wray knows you. How can she think you would do that?" Jack asked.

"It gets worse," Drake said.

"How?" Jack asked.

"I had to go and get that book from Mr. Zane. His room is next to Mrs. Wray's room," Drake said.

"I know that. But how does that make it worse?" Jack asked.

"I thought Mrs. Wray might be back from lunch. So I went to her door. And I looked into her room. Mr. Zane saw me. And he thinks I went into the room. But I didn't," Drake said.

"So that's why Mrs. Wray thinks you took your test," Jack said.

Drake said, "Yeah. And I have to prove to her that I didn't take it."

"How are you going to do that?" Jack asked.

"I don't know. Can you think of a way?" Drake asked.

"No, Drake. But I'll be glad to help

you. Just tell me what to do. And I'll do it," Jack said.

"Right now, I don't know what to do," Drake said.

"We need to hurry to class. But we can talk about this at lunch. And we'll think of something then," Jack said.

Drake hoped they would. But he wasn't so sure.

"Don't worry, Drake. We will find out who took your test," Jack said.

Drake hoped Jack was right. Jack had to be right. Or Drake was in big trouble.

Chapter 6

It was time for lunch. Drake hurried into the lunchroom. He got his tray. Then he looked for Logan and Jack.

He saw Logan. Logan was sitting with a girl. She was the girl Logan was trying to date. No one else was sitting with them. So Drake knew he shouldn't go over there.

Then Drake saw Jack. Jack was sitting with Lin, Paige, and Willow. The three girls lived at Grayson Apartments, too.

Drake went to their table, found a chair, and sat down.

He looked at Jack.

Drake asked, "Did you tell them?"

"No. I thought you would want to tell them yourself," Jack said.

"Tell us what?" the three girls asked at the same time.

Jack spoke before Drake could.

"Do you want me to ask Logan to come over here? So you can tell him, too. Just say the word. And I'll get him," Jack said.

"No. I'll tell him later," Drake said.

But Jack wanted to tell Logan.

"What do you have to tell us? We don't want to wait any longer to hear it," Paige said.

"My history test is missing. Someone took it," Drake said.

"Who?" the three girls asked at the same time.

"I don't know. But Mrs. Wray thinks I took it," Drake said.

Willow said, "How can she think that?

You were in math class."

"No. He wasn't," Jack said.

Drake didn't say anything.

The three girls looked at Jack. They all seemed surprised at what Jack said.

Then they looked at Drake.

"Why weren't you in math class?" Lin asked.

"And where were you?" Paige asked.

"One at a time. Give Drake a chance to answer," Willow said.

"I was in math class most of the time. But not all of the time," Drake said.

"Why weren't you there all of the time?" Paige asked.

"Miss Ortiz had asked me to get a book from Mr. Zane. But I forgot to get it. So Miss Ortiz sent me to get it during her class," Drake said.

Jack said, "Mr. Zane saw Drake. Drake was at Mrs. Wray's door. He was looking into her room. And Mrs. Wray wasn't there. Mr. Zane thought Drake went into the room. But he didn't."

"Why did you go to Mrs. Wray's door?" Lin asked.

"To find out if she'd graded my test," Drake said.

The five sat for a few minutes. And they didn't talk.

Then Willow said, "I don't think you took your test, Drake. But who else would want to take it?"

No one had an answer. So no one said anything.

Chapter 7

The five ate for a few minutes. They thought about what Willow had asked.

Then Jack asked, "Do you know someone who doesn't like you, Drake?"

"No. Do you?" Drake asked.

"No," Jack said.

Drake looked at Willow, Paige, and Lin. He said, "Do you know of someone?"

"No," the three girls said.

All of the students seemed to like Drake okay.

Willow said, "Coach Grant said you had to pass the test. And you had to take the test to him. You told us he said that. Who else did you tell?"

Drake said, "Just Caleb. He wanted to know what the coach said to me."

At first they all just ate some more. And they didn't talk.

Then Willow said, "I just thought of something."

"What?" the other four asked.

Willow said, "Caleb is the back-up quarterback. And he'll play if Drake doesn't play."

"Maybe Caleb took the test. So he can be the starting quarterback," Jack said.

Drake said, "Caleb didn't take my test. He wants me to play. He said I had to play, or we might lose. And he wants us to win."

"Did he say anything to you today about the test?" Paige asked.

Drake seemed surprised.

Drake said, "Yeah. Caleb asked me about it twice today."

"When?" Lin asked.

Drake said, "Before school. And then after history class. He said Mrs. Wray might not grade my test today. I told him she would grade it when she got back from lunch."

"Caleb took the test. That's for sure," Jack said.

"You don't know that Caleb took the test. So don't say that he did, Jack. But there might be a way we can find out," Willow said.

"How?" Drake asked.

Willow said, "We can find out what class Caleb had that period. And we can find out who his teacher is. Then one of us can go see his teacher. We can find out if Caleb was in class all period."

Drake said, "Caleb didn't have a class.

It was his lunch."

"No one would know where he was. He could've taken it. And then gone to lunch late," Paige said.

"Caleb took the test. That's for sure," Jack said again.

Willow didn't say anything to Jack that time.

Drake looked over at Jack.

Drake said, "You must be right after all, Jack. I can't believe Caleb would take my test. But he must have. He had time to do it. And no one else had a reason to take it."

"So what can we do about it, Jack?" Lin asked.

They all knew they had to do something. And soon. But what?

The five ate for a few minutes. And they didn't talk.

Then Willow said, "We need a plan."

"Just tell me what to do. And I'll do it," Jack said.

"What should we do first, Jack?" Lin asked.

"We need to find out if Caleb did take the test," Willow said.

"How can we do that?" Drake asked.

Then Paige said, "I have an idea."

"What?" Drake asked.

"Yes. What?" Jack asked.

Paige quickly told them her idea.

"That sounds like a plan to me," Drake said.

Drake got up from the table. He put his tray away. Then he hurried out of the lunchroom.

Chapter 8

Drake went to Mrs. Wray's room. It was almost time for her class to be over.

The bell rang. And Drake hurried to her room.

He hoped Mrs. Wray had found his test. And he hoped he and his friends were wrong about Caleb. But he didn't think they were.

Drake ran over to Mrs. Wray's room.

"Did you find my test, Mrs. Wray?" Drake asked.

Mrs. Wray said, "No, Drake. I didn't. I told you someone took it."

"I think I know who took my test," Drake said.

"Who?" Mrs. Wray asked.

"Caleb," Drake said.

Mrs. Wray said, "That's hard to believe, Drake."

Drake told her why he thought Caleb took the test.

Then Drake said, "I think I can prove it, Mrs. Wray. But I need your help."

Drake told Mrs. Wray what Paige's plan was. And Mrs. Wray said she would help Drake.

Drake wanted to talk to Caleb. But he had to go to his next class. So he would have to wait to talk to Caleb.

Drake hurried into his classroom. He hoped the class would go by quickly. And he was glad when the end of class bell rang.

Drake got his books. And he hurried out into the hall. He looked for Caleb. He saw Caleb. Caleb was walking down the hall.

Drake said, "Wait, Caleb."

Caleb stopped. He turned around. But he didn't seem glad to see Drake.

Caleb asked, "What do you want?"

"I have some great news," Drake said.

"What?" Caleb asked.

Drake didn't want to lie to Caleb. But he had to find out if Caleb took his test.

Drake said, "I passed my test. So I can play tonight."

Caleb seemed like he didn't quite believe Drake.

Caleb said, "How could Mrs. Wray grade your test? I thought your test was missing."

"Yeah. It is. But how did you know that?" Drake asked.

But Drake knew how Caleb knew. Caleb's face went very red.

"Someone told me," Caleb said.

"Who?" Drake asked.

"I don't know. You know how you just hear things," Caleb said.

"Yeah," Drake said.

"So how could Mrs. Wray grade your test?" Caleb asked.

"Mrs. Wray let me take it again," Drake said.

But that wasn't true.

"But you still have to take the test to Coach Grant. He said he had to see your test. Or you couldn't play," Caleb said.

Drake said, "I know. I'm going to take the test to him after school."

"Where's the test now?"

Drake said, "In Mrs. Wray's briefcase. She put it there after she graded it."

"Are you going to get your test right

after school?" Caleb asked.

"No. Mrs. Wray has a meeting with Mr. Zane. She said to wait about 15 minutes. And then to come and get it."

Caleb said, "Too bad you have to wait. I know you're in a hurry to get your test. So you can take it to Coach Grant."

Drake said, "Yeah. But I can use the time to go to the library."

Caleb got a big smile on his face.

Drake said, "I need to get to class. See you later."

Then Drake went to his next class.

Drake hoped the class would go by quickly. And he was glad when the school bell rang.

Drake hurried to where he could see Mrs. Wray's room. But it would be hard for other people to see him.

Drake saw Mrs. Wray walk out of her room. She went into Mr. Zane's room.

Drake saw Caleb. Caleb looked up and down the hall. Caleb didn't see Drake. Then Caleb quickly went into Mrs. Wray's room.

Drake hurried to Mr. Zane's room. Then he and Mrs. Wray went to Mrs. Wray's room. Mr. Zane followed them.

They saw Caleb. He was looking in Mrs. Wray's briefcase.

"What are you doing, Caleb?" Mrs. Wray asked.

"Yes, Caleb. What are you doing?" Mr. Zane asked.

But they knew what he was doing.

Drake said, "I took only one test, Caleb. The one you stole. What did you do with it?"

At first Caleb didn't want to say he took the test. But he knew they thought he took it.

Caleb pointed to a bookcase.

He said, "I put the test behind the bookcase."

Drake hurried over to the bookcase. He looked behind the bookcase. He could see some sheets of paper. Drake quickly got them from behind the bookcase. Drake looked at them.

"Is that your test, Drake?" Mr. Zane asked.

"Yes," Drake said.

Mr. Zane looked at Caleb.

Mr. Zane said, "This is a matter for Mr. Glenn. Come with me, Caleb. We'll go to his office."

Mr. Zane and Caleb walked out into the hall.

Drake walked over to Mrs. Wray. He gave his test to her.

Mrs. Wray said, "I'm glad you found your test, Drake. I'll grade it right now. So you can take it with you."

Mrs. Wray graded Drake's test. Then she said, "Good job, Drake. You got a B."

Now Drake could play in the big game. But Caleb wouldn't play in that game or in any more games at Carter High.